Karma's WORLD

THE GREAT SHINE-A-THON SHOWCASE!

Karma's WORLD

THE GREAT SHINE-A-THON SHOWCASE!

BY HALCYON PERSON

SCHOLASTIC INC.

The publisher does not have any control over and does not assume any responsibility for author or third-party websites or their content.

This book is a work of fiction. Names, characters, places, and incidents are either the product of the author's imagination or are used fictitiously, and any resemblance to actual persons, living or dead, business establishments, events, or locales is entirely coincidental.

Library of Congress Control Number Available

ISBN 978-1-338-58073-0

10 9 8 7 6 5 4 3 2 1   22 23 24 25 26

Printed in the U.S.A.   40

First printing 2022
Book design by Elliane Mellet
Illustrations by Yesenia Moises

FOR MY MOM, DAD, HANNIBAL, AND DAVE —
THANK YOU FOR ALWAYS SEEING MY SHINE,
EVEN WHEN I COULDN'T.

CHAPTER 1

"Winston! What are you doing?" Switch and I laughed so hard we practically fell off our seats in the cafeteria. But Winston just kept on dancing his ham sandwich across the table, singing along to his favorite song ever: MC Grillz's "High Roller Molar."

"I'm the hip hop dentist, best songs in the galaxy! / I be dancin', rappin', singin', savin' you from cavities!"

Winston sang and bounced his sandwich

back and forth on the table like little lunch dancers. Switch laughed so hard that juice came out of her nose!

As silly as it was, this was what I loved most about my best friends. Winston and I had been besties for forever. We grew up together in the neighborhood, and he knew everything about me—like that even though I might have rolled my eyes at his dancing sandwich routine, I still secretly loved it. We got to know Switch this year when she moved to Hansberry Heights with her mom. She may have been brand new when we met on the first day of fifth grade, but now we did everything together—playing soccer in the park, coming up with new dance moves at the Community Center, or just eating scones and slurping smoothies at the diner! All three of us were best friends, and we were always there for each other, no matter what. Plus, we always had so much fun—like, so much fun that juice came out of Switch's nose a lot 'cause we were always laughing so hard.

We were besties for lots of reasons, but one of them was that we all really loved hip hop. I wanted to grow up and be a rapper, and change the world with my music! And Switch, she was an amazing hip hop beat maker and music producer. She was gonna write all the music for my rhymes someday. Winston was a painter, a sculptor, a fashion designer—a little bit of everything, actually! He might not have known exactly what he was gonna do when he grew up, but I was sure whatever it was, it would be amazing.

Me, Winston, and Switch spent most of our time thinking about hip hop. And all three of us were MC Grillz's biggest fans—he was the coolest, most awesome rapper, and he had serious super swag. And just in case you were wondering, since he was a rapper and a dentist, all his songs were about teeth! We joined in with Winston as his sandwich danced down the table, singing the chorus of MC Grillz's first song together:

"If you wanna ride with me, just remember I don't play—every member of my crew is always brushin' twice a day!"

"Uhh . . . what are y'all doing?" Our giggles and Winston's sandwich dancing were interrupted by Crash and Chris, who slid into the seats next to us with their trays.

"Just practicing my moves for the concert this weekend," Winston shrugged, taking a bite from his dancer. "Gotta be ready for the show of the century!"

"No," Switch chimed in, eyes going wide. "The show of the millennium!"

"What show?" Chris asked, chowing down on his chicken nuggets. "What're you talking about?" Me, Winston, and Switch looked at each other before we all squealed together:

"The MC Grillz concert!" I didn't know

how Chris hadn't heard about it—practically everyone in our neighborhood was going to the concert this weekend. MC Grillz was coming to our city for the first time ever to put on a huge show. They said that it would have rapping, singing, dancing, and free toothbrushes for everyone!

And looking around the cafeteria, I could see that just about every kid at Peach Tree Middle School was going to be there—and all of them were just as excited as us. I saw Sam and Demi Ray in their MC Grillz tee shirts, doing his signature floss dance. I saw Megan and Sabiya typing on their laptops, getting updates on the latest MC Grillz concert news from fan websites. And Carrie, Danny, and Mateo were in the middle of a heated argument about which MC Grillz song was his best ever.

"'Toothpaste Be Poppin'!" Carrie said with a flip of her ponytail. "And that's final!"

"No way," Danny and Mateo replied. "It's gotta be 'Floss Like a Boss'!"

Looking around the cafeteria, I was getting even more excited for the concert. It seemed like everyone in the entire fifth grade was going, and we all couldn't wait to see MC Grillz in person!

"It's gonna be the best," I explained to Chris. "It's the biggest thing to happen to our neighborhood since, like, forever!"

"Yeah, dude," Crash added with his annoying smile. "Especially 'cause I have front row tickets." Crash pulled two super-shiny tooth-shaped tickets from his jacket pocket and waved them in front of Chris's face. "I'm gonna be so close to MC Grillz, he'll probably pull me up on stage to sing with him!"

Winston and Switch were impressed, but I couldn't help but roll my eyes. Crash was fine most of the time, I guess, but it felt like he always had to be the best at everything. He bragged all

the time! And sometimes I got competitive with him—especially when it was about music.

"Oh yeah?" I snapped back, "Well, me, Switch, and Winston are gonna get MC Grillz to pull *us* up on stage. 'Cause we're gonna have our own dance. And matching outfits! And . . . um . . . we're gonna do it all on roller skates!"

I could hear Winston leaning over to Switch to whisper, "Wait, we are?"

But Crash just smiled and popped one last tater tot into his mouth. "Yeah, sure—whatever,

Karma. I'll remember to wave to you when *I'm* up on stage, rapping with MC Grillz!" He laughed as he got up from the table and walked out of the cafeteria.

Ugh, Crash! He was always trying to be better than me! I knew then that we'd have to come up with a plan to get up on that stage so we were the ones waving to Crash . . . and not the other way around.

♪ ♫ ♪

"Um, Karm, are we *actually* gonna go to the concert on roller skates?" Winston asked nervously as we walked home from school. "'Cause I really, really can't roller skate."

I guess roller skates were off the table— but we had to do something special to get MC Grillz's attention at the concert! And even though Crash annoyed me, I wasn't gonna let our conversation with him stop me from being excited. Me, Switch, and Winston were just two days away from seeing MC Grillz in person, on stage, rapping all our favorite songs! We walked home from school that afternoon and talked through the plan for what was gonna be the best night of our lives.

To keep track of all our ideas, I pulled out my journal as we walked. I brought my journal everywhere with me—it was basically like my second brain. It's where I wrote my thoughts, feelings, and of course my rap lyrics. But right now, I was using it to plan our entire MC Grillz night, step by step. "So Winston, your abuelita will drop you off at my apartment at seven," I started writing.

"And my mom will bring me then, too!" Switch added.

"My dad will take us on the subway to the arena downtown," I said. "But how are we gonna get MC Grillz to notice us, so he pulls us up on stage? Ooh—maybe if we make matching tee shirts with his face on them!"

"And we could come up with a special dance for his new song," Switch suggested.

"And we should definitely bring pickle chips." Winston tapped my journal page seriously. "I heard they are MC Grillz's favorite snack!"

We all giggled as I wrote it down. "Pickle chips—got it," I said.

"Did somebody say pickle chips?!" Running from the entrance of his school, my little brother Keys butted his way into our conversation, just like he always did. Pickle chips just so happened to be his favorite snack, too—he was basically obsessed with them. He was holding another one of his super silly inventions in his hands. He made them all the time from random things around our apartment. But whatever that thing did, I didn't want it anywhere near me—Keys's last invention had blasted pudding all over my bedroom!

"I should probably go to the concert, so I can talk to MC Grillz about our favorite snack," Keys said.

"Keys, Mom and Dad told you already. You're too young to come to the concert with us," I explained. "It's past your bedtime, remember?" But Keys just waved me off with a grin and held up his funny-looking machine.

"Psh, I made an invention to fix that!" It sort of looked like a bicycle helmet, but with all kinds

of things sticking out of it—light bulbs, paint brushes . . . and was that my dad's spatula? "It's my Grower-Upper-Mizer! It'll make me older—old enough to come to the concert with you!"

Keys put on the helmet and started to press buttons.

"Ohhh no! Keep that thing away from me!" I said, stepping back and pulling Winston and Switch with me. "Last time you did this, I had pudding on my pillows for a week."

But Keys just kept pressing buttons confidently. "Karma, you worry too much! Just watch, when I take this helmet off, I'll be all grown up!" Then suddenly, the helmet started making all sorts of funny noises. There was a beep, a squeak, and even a fart as Keys started spinning out of control around the sidewalk!

"Uh oh," he said under the helmet. "Get this thing offa me!" Obviously, Keys's latest invention was not working the way he wanted it to—no surprise there.

"Whoaaa-aaaa-aaaaaah!" he yelled as he spun this way, that way, then finally crashed into the bushes next to our stoop. When he popped out of the leaves, we saw that his helmet had painted a very silly, twirly mustache across his face.

"Heh . . . do I look all grown up?" Keys asked dizzily as me and Winston laughed and helped him out of the bushes.

"Nope, not yet," I said. "Maybe if you try painting on a whole beard?"

Keys glared at me as I giggled and walked up the stoop steps to our apartment. "C'mon Win, Switch—let's go up to my room and keep planning for the MC Grillz concert!"

But when we walked into my apartment, I could feel something wasn't right. My mom and dad were both on the couch, waiting for us—and they had that look in their eyes that told me whatever they were gonna say next definitely wasn't gonna be good.

★ 13 ★

"Kar-Star . . . we have some news," my dad said, calling me over to the couch next to him.

"You know the MC Grillz concert this weekend?" my mom said.

"Ooh yeah!" Switch clapped. "We're gonna make matching tee shirts, and come up with dance moves—"

"And get pulled up on stage to sing with him!" Winston added excitedly.

But I wasn't excited. "Dad, what's wrong?"

My dad sighed and shook his head. "The MC Grillz concert has been canceled."

CHAPTER 2

"Canceled?!" I was so surprised that I almost fell over onto Major, my dog, who was sleeping curled up on the rug. "But how can they cancel the show?"

"We just saw it on the news. Turns out MC Grillz's tour bus broke down on his way across the country," Mom explained. "Looks like he won't be able to make it to Hansberry Heights in time for the show." I could feel my eyes start to fill with tears. How could this be happening? "Come here, baby." She pulled me in for a hug, which made me feel a little better. My mom gives the best hugs in the entire world.

But before I could squeeze her back, I felt Winston's arms around me, too! He joined us for a big group hug, which he's been doing ever since we were just little kids. "I need a hug, too!" he wailed, totally dramatic. I could tell Winston might be feeling even worse than I was about the MC Grillz news.

Switch picked up our remote and turned on the TV. On it, a reporter was standing in front of the big concert arena where MC Grillz was supposed to perform this weekend.

"Breaking news: MC Grillz has just announced that he will be canceling his performance this Sunday in Hansberry Heights because of engine trouble on his tour bus, nicknamed the 'Brush Bus.'" A picture of a giant toothbrush-themed bus appeared on screen.

RAP SUPERSTAR MC GRILLZ STRANDED
HANSBERRY HEIGHTS CONCERT CANCELED

5:15 PM
85°F

"MC Grillz explained to reporters that while a toothbrush-themed bus seemed like a good idea at the start of his tour, it's caused nothing but trouble."

They played a clip of MC Grillz from his website. In it, he was talking into his phone camera while he pushed on the back of his giant bus. "Aw, man! This thing has been a mess since day one!" No matter how hard he pushed, he couldn't get the bus to move. "First the bristles start flyin' off, and now the engine's broken!"

He started pushing the bus again, but no luck. He looked back at his camera. "Sorry, Hansberry Heights. There's no way to get to you by train, or by boat, and . . ." He gulped. "I'm afraid to fly! So . . . I don't think I'm gonna make it."

Switch clicked off the TV and looked back at me sadly. "We've been planning for this concert for months . . . and now it's just canceled?"

I didn't want to believe it. I couldn't believe it! I thought about all our exciting plans—our matching tee shirts, our awesome dance moves. Now, we'd never get pulled up on stage by MC Grillz. We'd never even get to see him perform at all.

I looked over at my besties. Winston was still hugging my mom and wailing something I couldn't understand. And in classic Switch mode, she was already trying to figure out how to fix things. "But there's got to be a way to get MC Grillz here in time for the show. Maybe we could send a different bus to get him here! Or what if we got him a helicopter? Or a blimp? Or a submarine? Or or or—"

Dad shook his head sadly. "Sorry, Switch, but I just don't think there's any way that'll work." He paused, then added, "Plus . . . I think submarines only work underwater."

I realized that there really, truly was no way for us to get MC Grillz here in time for the concert. The best night of our lives was now . . . canceled.

"Sorry, Kar-Star," my dad said. "Is there anything that would cheer you up?" I gave Switch and Winston a nod. When we were feeling sad, there was only one thing to do.

♪ ♫ ♪

We always went to the Community Center to play foosball when we were feeling down. Like that time our soccer team lost a game by just one goal. Or that time a pigeon flew down and ate Winston's triple-scoop chunko-chocolate ice cream cone. But this time, our sadness was way bigger than stolen ice cream. And something told me that even if we played a million foosball games, nothing could make us feel better right now. And when we walked into the Community Center, I learned I was right.

Inside, I saw all my friends from school who had been excited about MC Grillz. I saw Sam and Demi Ray sadly pulling off their MC Grillz tee shirts, no longer dancing. I saw Sabiya and Megan glumly closing their laptops, no longer searching for the latest Grillz news. And Carrie, Mateo, and Danny were all sitting heartbroken on the center's steps, no longer arguing about MC Grillz's best song. Actually, they weren't saying anything at all. Soon they stood up and came into the Community Center.

And it wasn't just kids from school. It looked

like the whole community had heard the news about MC Grillz! I saw some of the high school kids complaining by the bean bag chairs. And over by the TV set, I saw some adults watching the news report about MC Grillz and the Brush Bus with disappointment on their faces. I even saw our teacher, Mr. Singal, singing a slow, sad version of "Toothpaste Be Poppin'" and strumming along with his guitar. It wasn't the best version of the song . . . but it sounded about as bad as we all felt.

So even though he got on my nerves sometimes, I couldn't help but feel kinda sorry for Crash when I spotted him and Chris walking in. I could tell that they'd heard the news, too. "I can't believe it, man." Crash was shaking his head. "I had front row tickets and everything!"

"Sorry, dude," Chris replied, putting his arm around Crash's shoulder. "But look on the bright side—now on Sunday you can just sit at home and think about how cool the concert woulda been if you'd actually gotten to go!" There was a pause, then Chris added, "Wait, I guess that actually doesn't sound very fun. That sounds terrible."

Crash rolled his eyes at Chris before spotting me across the center. We shook our heads at each other sadly. Even though Crash could be annoying, I got how he felt. We were all really sad about MC Grillz.

"What's with this gloomy roomy?" All of a sudden my grumpy downstairs neighbor, Mr. Crawford, walked into the main room of the Community Center. He must've seen how down we all were, because he asked, "Did Winston's ice cream cone get eaten by a pigeon again?"

But before Mr. Crawford could grab his pigeon-shooing broom, Winston stopped him. "No, Mr. Crawford—this rapper we all really like was supposed to perform a big concert this weekend . . . but we just found out that his show is canceled." He looked around the room at all the sad faces. "We're all takin' it pretty hard."

Mr. Crawford gasped, his eyes going wide. "Do you mean MC Grillz? His concert was canceled?"

"Wait, you know who MC Grillz is?" Sabiya asked. It was a good question—Mr. Crawford didn't really seem like your typical MC Grillz fan. But then he started singing one of his biggest songs, "Floss Like a Boss."

If you floss erryday, then you can ride with me! Get up in between yo teeth, to prevent those cavities! Floss like a boss, floss like a boss!"

Winston's mouth just about dropped to the floor as Mr. Crawford started doing MC Grillz's signature floss dance. Was it actually possible that Mr. Crawford was as big a fan of MC Grillz as we were?

"You bet your bristles I'm an MC Grillz fan," Mr. Crawford said. "I can't believe his concert was canceled." Just like us, Mr. Crawford was really disappointed. He slumped into a seat near an equally sad Carrie and Danny.

Looking around the Community Center, it seemed like my whole neighborhood was sad, and I was, too. When I felt like this, there was only one thing for me to do. I found a quiet corner away from all the people, the noises, and the distractions. And then I took out my pen, and my journal . . . and I started to write.

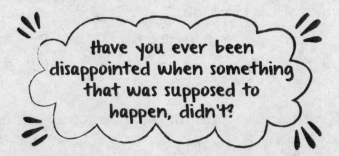

Have you ever been disappointed when something that was supposed to happen, didn't?

Well, that's how me and my friends feel right now. Me, Winston, and Switch just found out that the MC Grillz concert was canceled this weekend. Sunday was supposed to be the best night of our lives! We were all so excited that MC Grillz was gonna come to our city . . . and now all our dreams of seeing him are gone. I feel sad, frustrated, disappointed . . . and most of all, I just wish there was

a way I could help make everyone feel better.

It's wild, I can't believe what went an'

happened today

This mornin' we were happy, plannin' away

For the MC Grillz concert, best night of our lives

But little did we know we were in for a surprise

MC Grillz isn't comin', he's stuck outta town

And now me, Winston, Switch, we can't get ridda

these frowns

Broken-down bus, our whole community's crushed

The MC Grillz show meant so much to all of us

I just wish there was a way I could make things better

I wanna show my 'hood that we'll get through it together

So what if the Grillz show has been totally blown

Maybe . . . we should put on a concert of our own?

Wait, that's it! What if . . . we did our own concert instead?

"What if we did our own concert instead?!" Before I knew it, I was shouting out loud the same thing I'd just written in my journal. Everyone in the entire Community Center turned to look at me, a confused look on all their faces.

"What do you mean, Karm?" Switch asked, joining me. Around me, the other kids were gathering, too. I stepped up onto my chair and looked out over the entire Center.

"MC Grillz was supposed to perform

Sunday, right?" I said as my friends nodded. "Well, just because his Brush Bus broke down, that doesn't mean we can't still have a show!"

Crash scoffed, waving me away in that annoying way he always does. "Psh, MC Grillz isn't here, and he definitely won't be here by Sunday." Around him, other kids mumbled in agreement, getting disappointed all over again. "So who exactly are you suggesting is gonna perform at this little concert?"

"Well . . . what about all of us?" I said with a big smile. Around me, the entire Community Center went silent.

At that moment, it felt like time froze. I could feel my heartbeat thumping all the way up in my ears. Was this a bad idea? Was I being silly? Was I about to embarrass myself in front of everyone? But even though I was nervous that I might be wrong, I tightened my fists and kept explaining. I knew that what I had to say was important.

"We don't need MC Grillz. We've got talents,

and skills. So, what if we put on our own show to cheer up the whole neighborhood?" I asked. Next to me, I could see Winston and Switch begin to smile. They were starting to like my idea!

"Karma's right! We can all do what we're good at," Winston jumped in, stepping up onto the chair beside me. "We'll work together to put on a show even better than the MC Grillz concert!" Some of my classmates were smiling, nodding, starting to see what we meant. But others still looked unsure.

"But, Karma . . . ?" Demi Ray, who could be kinda shy and quiet sometimes, pushed her hand up into the air like she was asking a question in science class. "How can we put on a whole concert? We're just kids." It seemed like they were worried that just 'cause we were fifth graders, we couldn't plan a whole concert ourselves.

"Well . . ." I hesitated, losing my confidence. Maybe she was right? But then I looked back at Winston, who gave me a supportive smile. "What do you really need for a concert?"

"Music, for one." Crash crossed his arms, rolling his eyes at my question.

"And dancers?" Sam added.

"Ooh, and we'd need to sell tickets, and get everyone in the neighborhood to come," Megan jumped in.

"We'll need costumes," Danny added.

"And maybe an awesome stage, with all sorts of cool sets?" Tommie offered.

"And what about an epic laser show with smoke machines and a giant robot dragon who breathes fire!" Chris, getting way too excited, started air guitaring as we all giggled at his silly answer.

"Well, I dunno about the giant fire-breathing robot dragon . . ." I started, looking back at my friends. "But who says we can't do everything else ourselves?" I pointed to Sam and Demi Ray. "You both know the 'Floss Like a Boss' dance moves by heart." I pointed to Sabiya and Megan. "And you two can totally design a website to sell tickets, and let everyone in the whole neighborhood know about the show!"

Winston nodded. "And I can make a really cool set here at the Community Center! I'll paint it myself!"

Carrie and Danny jumped up. "And we can make costumes for everyone!"

It was working! But then, Crash interrupted.

"Yeah, Karma . . . that's all chill. But what about music? You really think you're as good a rapper as MC Grillz?" Crash curled up his mouth in that frustrating smile he always had when he thought he was right.

"I'm not saying that. And I'm not saying I'll rap all by myself," I told Crash. "We can all sing songs. We can play instruments, or do magic tricks!" There was another pause as everyone in the crowd looked at one another, then back at me.

"Can I do my one-handed cartwheel?" Sam asked, getting excited. "I love doing cartwheels."

"And can we do skateboard tricks? We've been practicing." Danny spoke up, putting his arm around Tommie.

"Ooh! Ooh! And can I do knock-knock jokes?" Chris asked. "Like, here's one of my favorites: Knock, knock. Who's there? Giant fire-breathing robot dragon. Giant fire-breathing robot dra—"

I laughed, interrupting Chris. "As much as I wanna hear how that joke ends, you should save it for the show!" I turned back to my friends, getting more excited with every word. "We should all perform—and we should all do whatever we love. Whatever makes you shine!"

"'Shine'?" Crash replied sarcastically. "What are you even talking about, Karma?"

I paused for a second. Crash's question was a good one. What did it mean to shine, really? "Well . . ." I started, not exactly sure how I was going to answer. "I feel like I'm shining when I'm doing something I love . . . and I'm having fun doing it." I turned and smiled at Winston and Switch. "Like when me, Winston, and Switch are in the cafeteria, rapping and making beats . . . and making a sandwich dance!"

Then I turned back to my other friends. "But everyone can shine their own way! As long as you're doing what you love, and having fun—it'll be the best concert ever."

"That's right!" Switch added, stepping up onto a chair next to me and Winston, joining our team. "If we do Karma's idea, we can all have a chance to shine for the whole neighborhood!"

And that's when it hit me—I knew what we had to call our show!

"It'll be the SHINE-A-THON SHOWCASE!" I

cheered, throwing my hands up into the air. "The show where every kid in Hansberry Heights gets to shine!"

Suddenly it felt like the whole Community Center was buzzing with excitement—everyone was in, and wanted to perform! It seemed like they were all already planning how they were going to add to the big show. Then, my eyes landed on Crash, who seemed to be the only person not happy about the Shine-A-Thon Showcase. Actually . . . he looked a little upset! As he put his head down and walked away from the crowd, I got a little worried. What was goin' on with him?

But I couldn't think about Crash now. I had a whole show to organize! And as I looked at my besties standing next to me, I knew we could do this. I smiled big and pulled them in for a warm hug. "Woohoo! We're doin' it! We're putting on a concert!"

And that's when, still squished in my hug, Switch reminded me of something I hadn't thought about before with a nervous giggle. "Heh, yeah, Karma . . . and we only have two days to do it!"

CHAPTER 3

Switch was right—we had to get to work right away if we were going to pull off the Shine-A-Thon Showcase by Sunday night! We left the Community Center and headed back to my apartment to plan. "It'll be Shine-A-Thon Central," I said, smiling at my friends. "We can use my apartment to organize the whole concert!"

As we walked home, I started writing in my journal again, taking down Winston and

Switch's ideas. "We'll need to come up with jobs for everyone," Switch started, already thinking about who could do what.

"Ooh! I can't wait to design the set for the show," Winston said. "I can paint it to look like a bright star—like we're all shining!"

Switch and I both loved that idea. "That's great. You'll be so good at that!"

"And I can be the producer," Switch said. "I'll organize the music, and the lights, and make sure that everything's running on time."

Winston and I both smiled big. "Yes! That's the perfect job for you!" I smiled at Switch. "You're basically the best planner I know."

Then Winston started rattling off other jobs for our friends: "Sam and Demi Ray could come up with all the choreography . . . and maybe Danny and Carrie could handle the costumes? Who else, who else . . ."

"How about *me*?!" Once again Keys interrupted our conversation as we turned onto our block. It was like he had a special sensor for when we were doing serious and important things, so he could come annoy us. I rolled my eyes as he skipped along with us down the sidewalk.

"Keys, you really wanna be a part of the Shine-A-Thon Showcase? How are you gonna help?"

"Psh, I already started helping!" Keys responded, pulling something from his backpack. It looked like a giant . . . pickle? It was made out of metal, it was the size of a suitcase, and seemed like it was held together with screws, tape, and peanut butter.

"It's my PICKLE POWERED SHINE BLASTER!" Keys cheered.

The three of us blinked. Keys acted like we should know exactly what a "pickle powered shine blaster" is. "What . . . does it do, exactly?" Winston asked.

"Well, when I finish, it's gonna blast all the

coolest lights, and sounds—it'll even make cool smoke for the concert!" Keys pulled his screwdriver from the side pocket of his backpack. Then he stuck it into the pickle as we kept walking, fixing something inside. "It'll be the perfect thing to light your show, Karma!"

I raised an eyebrow at my little brother. That *did* sound pretty cool . . . but knowing Keys's inventions, it might just as easily blast pickle juice as lights and sounds. "And you can really make it work in only two days?" That seemed like a stretch, even for a kid who made a Pudding Blaster out of a vacuum and Mom's old sponges.

"Of course I can!" Keys said confidently. Without missing a beat he spun his bright red screwdriver around on his finger. "With my lucky screwdriver, I can do anything!"

At first I wanted to tell Keys to leave us alone, but I had to admit, inventing was the way that Keys shined. So if the Shine-A-Thon Showcase was all about the kids in our neighborhood showing off their talents, inventing a shining pickle was the perfect way for him to help!

"Alright," I said, giving Keys a squeeze. "That sounds pretty fun. We can use it to kick off the show!"

"So that means . . ." Switch looked over my shoulder at my journal page to see the list I was making. "We've got kids to make costumes, set up the lights, do the music . . ." And as she continued, I started to wonder:

"But … what am I gonna do?" I asked. It seemed like every single person had a cool job except for me. Switch was producing, and Winston was designing the stage. Even Keys was involved by inventing something!

"What?! Are you kidding, Karm?" Switch elbowed me playfully and laughed. "You've got the biggest job of all. You're our director!"

"You have to plan all the performances. Like who does what, and when!" Winston said.

"The director's the glue that brings the whole show together," Switch explained. Wow, me? A director? I'd never been a director before.

"And the first thing you need to decide is what we're going to do for the opening number—the big song to start the Shine-A-Thon! It has to be epic, to show everyone that we can pull off something as awesome as an MC Grillz concert."

I took a deep breath. Part of me was really excited about having all that responsibility and getting to make all those decisions for our show.

But another part of me was kind of nervous. What if I wasn't good at it?

I think Switch could tell I was getting a little nervous. She elbowed me again as we walked up the steps of my stoop. "You got this, Karm," she said with a warm smile. "If you can figure out how to add Keys's pickle shine blaster to our show, you can do anything."

Winston nodded. "And me and Switch'll be here to help you, no matter what."

CHAPTER 4

Winston and Switch's confidence in me really made me feel better. They were right; I could totally do this! And I wasn't alone if I had my besties right beside me to help. The Shine-A-Thon Showcase was gonna be the most amazing concert Hansberry Heights had ever seen!

So the next morning when I woke up, I wasn't feeling nervous anymore—I was feeling excited. Today was the day we started rehearsing for the Shine-A-Thon Showcase! I looked out the window and saw that the sun was beaming down on all the pretty rooftops across my neighborhood. In the distance I could hear the sound of the train passing on the high tracks, rumbling toward downtown. As I sniffed the air, I could smell Dad's cornbread baking—my favorite! Yep, it seemed like it was gonna be a pretty great day.

Just then, Major came running into my room and jumped up onto my bed, giving me early morning kisses. And suddenly, I wasn't smelling delicious cornbread anymore . . . I was smelling his nasty morning breath! But I didn't mind—I giggled and gave him a scratch behind the ear, just like he likes.

I stretched my arms super far and super wide, letting out a big, happy yawn. Then I took off my bonnet, got dressed, and made my bed. Yep, today we were gonna plan the Shine-A-Thon Showcase—and I just knew it was gonna be a great day!

But then . . . I went downstairs.

There, on my dining room table, it looked like all of Winston's art supplies had exploded. He was lost in his own world, painting a giant canvas with strokes of bright colors that were splattering everywhere. "Winston, what is all this? My mom's gonna—"

"Bup bup bup!" He put a finger up in the air to me as he continued looking at his painting. "Artist at work—please do not disturb!" I rolled my eyes at him as he continued to drip paint all over.

But I couldn't focus on Winston's mess for very long, because in the kitchen, Keys was wheeling his wagon to the cupboard. I watched as he opened up our cabinets and took out a bag of pickle chips. Then another, and another. Pretty soon, he'd placed dozens of bags of chips down on the counter. He started opening them one by one and pouring them into his wagon, creating a giant pile of chips.

"What are you doing?" I asked as Keys crunched down on a chip. "Pickle chips for breakfast? Really?"

Keys just shrugged. "Yep! They're brain food. They help me invent!"

From the dining room, I heard Winston yell: "Ooh! Can I have some?"

"But why are you putting all these chips in your wagon?" I asked, still totally confused by what my weird little brother was doing.

"I'm prepping for two BIG days of inventing," he responded, crunching on another chip. "I'm gonna need all the pickle power I can get." He patted the metal side of his pickle invention. "And so is my invention! It's pickle chip–powered, of course."

Keys was totally ridiculous. But before I could worry too much about his silly plan, Switch marched through the living room. She was writing frantically on a clipboard and speaking fast into a walkie-talkie. "Sabiya, do you have eyes on Danny? Over!"

From her walkie-talkie, I could hear Sabiya's voice squawk back. "Yes, I see him now— he's got the costumes and he's heading over. Over!"

But before Switch could answer her, Sabiya added: "Wait, do I say 'over' twice if my sentence already ends with 'over'? How does that work?"

Switch looked up at me and shook her head as Sabiya kept talking. "And why *do* we say 'over,' anyway? I wanna say, 'Sabiya… OUT!' Doesn't that sound cooler, Mateo?" We heard Mateo's muffled voice respond, but Switch interrupted impatiently.

"Just let me know when the costumes are ready to try on, okay?" Switch said, pinching her nose in that way she does when she's kinda stressed out.

"Okay!" Sabiya responded. "Sabiya . . . OUT!" I couldn't help but giggle at my silly friends, but Switch was all business. Before I could even get a piece of my dad's cornbread, she sat me down in front of a long to-do list. Like, so long it went from the dining room table all the way down to the floor.

"Karma, we have a lot to do. Like, a lot a lot. And since you're the director . . ." Switch gave me a nervous look. "You have to make the decisions." She tapped the top of the to-do list. "And first things first—we have to decide what we're doing for the big open, to start the show."

Part of me wanted to walk right back up the stairs to my room and get back into bed with Major and his stinky breath. But before I could tell Switch this, we had another, even bigger, problem on our hands. Suddenly Keys was all up in our grill. He was looking under the table, under my feet, under the rug. Then, he walked right up to me and lifted up my left arm to look under that!

"Excuse you?" I said as he dropped my arm and kept searching, frantically rushing into the kitchen to open all the cupboard doors again and then pulling out all the drawers. "What is going on, Keys?"

"My lucky screwdriver! I can't find it!" As Major lazily trotted down the stairs and curled up on his dog bed, Keys rushed over to pick him up and search under him, too. "Without it, I can't fix things, or build things . . . I can't invent at all!" He held up his pickle invention with a worried look on his face. "And I won't be able to finish my Pickle Powered Shine Blaster!"

Keys, not inventing? That was like MC Grillz not rapping about toothbrushes. Me and Winston's eyes both went wide in surprise. "No way—you can still invent!" I walked over to our family's junk drawer and pulled another screwdriver from it. I held it out to Keys. "Here, take this one."

But Keys just shook his head. "No, nope, no way, never!" Before I could stop him, he started pulling cushions up off our couch and shaking them, still searching. "I can't invent with just any ol' screwdriver. I need my lucky one! I won't be able to help with the Shine-A-Thon Showcase 'til I find it!"

Inventing was his whole life. He had to find that screwdriver—not just for our show, but because it's what he loved to do.

Just then, Mom walked in with groceries and saw our apartment. And the look on her face told me she was not too happy. Between Winston's messy painting and Keys's frantic searching, the place looked like a disaster.

"Winston Torres, I know you are not dripping paint all over my house," she said, dropping her bags onto the window seat as she walked toward Winston. "And Keys Lamont Grant, what are my couch cushions doing on the floor?" Winston and Keys stopped in their tracks and looked up at her with embarrassed smiles. All I could think was *oops*.

Mom walked over to me, confused. "What is this? What are y'all doin' to my dining room?"

"Mom, I know it's messy . . . but it's for a good reason! We're doing a concert tomorrow. It's called the Shine-A-Thon Showcase!" I tried to explain. "Since MC Grillz can't be here, we thought we'd put on a show for the neighborhood ourselves. We're all gonna do what we love, and we're gonna have a lot of fun. It's so every kid can shine!"

I could tell right away that my mom liked that idea. But did she like it enough to not get mad about this big mess? She smiled at me. "That's so exciting, Kar-Star. I'm proud of you. I know it'll be a lot of work, but you're doing something so nice for our community." I breathed a sigh of relief.

"But Mr. Torres"—my mom turned to Winston as another glob of paint fell off his brush and onto the floor—"you're gonna clean up this mess, you hear?" She handed him a sponge. "And Keys?" Keys gave her that sweet smile he always tried when she was about to give him a chore. "I know by the time I finish unpacking these groceries, those couch cushions will be back where they belong."

Finally, she handed a rag to me and some spray cleaner to Switch. "And you can help." Before we could complain, she gave me a wink and a grin. "Get to shinin'."

But it turned out that cleaning up Winston's paint was gonna be the easiest thing we did all day. Once we got the splatters off the table, the floor, the rug—there was even some on Major's tail!—Switch tapped my to-do list with her pencil. "C'mon, director—everyone's waiting for us at the Community Center! And they need you to make decisions, now."

CHAPTER 5

When we walked into the Community Center, it was like we'd walked right into the backstage of a concert. Everywhere I looked, I saw kids from my neighborhood working on getting the show ready. The place was buzzing with excitement: I heard lots of talking and then, when things got too loud, yelling. I heard the squeaks and squawks of instruments being tuned and Mr. Crawford telling kids not to scuff up his nice clean floor.

While me, Switch, and Winston watched the messy chaos, we saw Tommie and Chris running across the stage carrying armfuls of jangly tambourines. In one corner, Sabiya and Megan were setting up a whole website for our show. In another, Carrie and Danny were organizing a rack of clothing. I could make out purple feathers, sparkly sequins, and a stack of astronaut's helmets. Mateo cut through the Center, pushing a big box piled with colorful, furry puppets across the floor. What in the world were we gonna be doing with a giant box of puppets?

Then, I heard Demi Ray's voice: "And five, six, seven, eight!" She and Sam were hard at work on a dance routine at center stage, pumping their fists and jumping to a hip hop jam. But Demi Ray was so into it that she jumped too high and knocked into Sam, who knocked into Carrie, who knocked into that giant box of puppets! We heard a crash, a bang, and then a thud as she fell inside the box.

After a second, I saw Carrie's head, ponytail and all, pop up from the pile of fuzzy puppets around her. "Ughhhh!"

Mateo rushed over. "Oh no! Are you okay?"

Carrie stood up and brushed herself off. "Yeah, I'm fine. I just—"

But Mateo was ignoring Carrie. He rushed to one of the puppets that had fallen over and squeezed its green fur. "I was so worried about you!"

Carrie rolled her eyes. Then suddenly, Keys's head popped out of the puppet pile next to her! I wasn't expecting that. "Nope, my lucky screwdriver isn't in here, either," he said, shaking his head.

I could see that all of my friends had gotten

right to work on the concert. Which made sense, 'cause it was happening tomorrow night! As soon as everyone spotted me, they all rushed over and started asking a million questions, all at once.

"Karma, you're the director—so we need you to look at these costumes. The thrift store only had these two looks. So do you like the purple feathers better, or the astronaut costume?" Carrie said, holding up two extremely different costumes for our show.

"Umm . . ." But before I could even answer, I heard another voice.

"Karma, Karma—what do you think of this saxophone solo?" Taking a big, deep breath, Tommie blew as hard as he could into his saxophone, making a honk so loud that you could probably hear it in space.

But I couldn't even concentrate on Tommie's very loud solo, 'cause Switch was tapping her clipboard at me again. "And we still need a decision about the big opening number, Karm. What do you think?"

Before I could answer her, Chris stuck his head close to me with another question. "Karma, I decided I'm done with knock-knock jokes—now I'm thinking about burping the alphabet. Thoughts?" Then he started burping so loud, it sounded like an earthquake. "*AAAA!! BBBB!! CCCCCC!!!!*"

It felt like time froze. All around me more and more voices started asking me to make all sorts of decisions. I know that's what a director is supposed to do, but as I looked from the purple-y feather-y jackets to the astronaut helmets, I couldn't decide. "Umm . . . well . . . I'm not sure . . . Can I have a second to . . ." I felt like there was a super-bright, super-hot spotlight shining down on just me, and everyone was waiting for me to mess up. My eyes darted 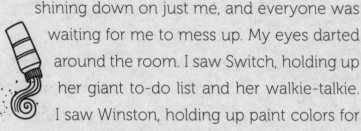 around the room. I saw Switch, holding up her giant to-do list and her walkie-talkie. I saw Winston, holding up paint colors for me to choose between. I saw costumes, and instruments, and puppets, and dance moves, and somehow, Chris was still burping the alphabet at me! Finally, I just shouted:

"EVERYBODY, STOP!" I was so loud that the whole Community Center went quiet. Even Chris stopped burping as his mouth dropped in shock.

"Excuse you! Inside voice!" Mr. Crawford called from his perch in the reading nook. As everyone stared at me I rubbed my arm, feeling embarrassed. I just needed to be alone. I just needed a minute to think. I needed to write things down in my journal.

"Um, I'll be right back." I needed a minute to myself to figure out what I was gonna do next—and I knew just where to go. I grabbed my backpack and ran up the stairs of the Community Center.

I pushed through the loud metal door to the rooftop of the Community Center. It was a pretty normal roof—just boring old concrete. But I loved being up here because of the view. From here, I could see my whole neighborhood. The cars and buses, the park, and Peach Tree Middle School. I could even see my apartment. I left the door open a crack and slid down to sit, my back against the cement wall.

I let out the biggest sigh ever. It was finally quiet, and I felt like I could think again. I took out my journal, and started to write.

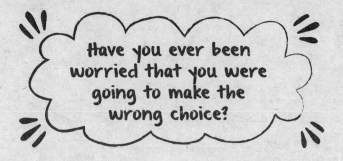

Have you ever been worried that you were going to make the wrong choice?

'Cause that's how I feel right now. When I came up with the idea for the Shine-A-Thon Showcase, I thought it would be so much fun. Just me, and my friends, putting on a big show for our whole neighborhood.

But now it feels like I'm under so much pressure to make the right choices. Because I'm the director, everyone needs me to make decisions—what we'll wear, what we'll sing, what dance moves we'll do, even what puppets we'll use! It's up to me to make sure things are perfect. And if I choose wrong, the whole concert will be ruined.

The whole point of the show was for all of us kids to shine—and if I don't do things just right, everyone's gonna be disappointed. What if I make the wrong choice? What if I mess up?

I'm feelin' so much pressure, and I don't know what to do

My friends are countin' on me, but can I really come through?

I'm the director, I'm s'posed to step up and make a choice

But when I wanna say my mind, it's like I lose my voice!

So much to do, so many choices to make

And if I choose wrong? Then it's my mistake

Should we dress like astronauts?

Put on purple feathers?

I can't decide, why can't I pick which one is better?

The Shine-A-Thon is coming, only one day away

If I don't step up, there won't be a show Sunday

I wanted all of us to shine, but now I've got doubts

Maybe these lights are about to go out?

Just then, the strangest sound broke through the silence on the roof. I looked up in surprise, accidentally drawing a line across my journal. What was that? It sounded like . . . was that someone singing?

"Shine, shine, shine! Shine brighter than the sun! / Together, we're better, all of us over one! / We are starlight, we shine so bright, each of us have our place! / But when we come together you can see us shine from space!"

It was a voice . . . a voice I recognized, but couldn't quite figure out. And it was singing the coolest song—a song I'd never heard before! My head started bouncing to the beat of it. It was catchy, and made me want to sing along. It sounded really, really good! And whoever it was, they were on the other side of the wall. But as I stepped toward the singing voice, the door creaked loudly again. Suddenly, the voice stopped singing.

"Hello? Who's up here?" Just then, the person behind the voice revealed themselves, walking around the side of the wall. "Karma?"

I couldn't believe it . . . the voice was Crash!

CHAPTER 6

Crash stood in front of me, looking embarrassed. "Uhh . . . can we pretend you didn't just hear that?"

But I was too shocked to hear what he was saying. "Crash, you sounded so good! Like, incredible! Like, amazing!"

Crash rolled his eyes at me. "That doesn't sound like you pretending not to have heard."

"What was that song? What were you singing?"

There was a pause as Crash looked out at the view of our neighborhood. He took a deep breath, then sighed, like he was deciding to finally reveal a big secret. "Well, you know how I sing opera music?" Crash said, and I nodded. At school there had been a day where we had to go up and tell the class what our dream job was. I wanted to be a rapper, of course—and even though he was nervous about it at first, Crash eventually told us he wanted to be an opera singer.

"So recently, I've been trying this new thing. I've been trying to write my own songs . . . sorta like you do." Crash looked up to me, a small smile spreading across his face. But then his smile was replaced by panic as he remembered what he'd just told me. "But you can't tell anyone about it! It's not ready!"

Crash? Writing songs? I never thought he'd want to do something like that. But I had to admit, what I'd heard was pretty good. "So you wrote: *Shine, shine, shine! Shine brighter than the sun!*" I sang it back to him, and his eyes widened.

"You . . . you remember it?"

I nodded. "Of course. It's really catchy."

"Thanks." Even though Crash didn't say much, and looked away right when he said it, I could tell my compliment meant a lot to him. He focused on his sneakers, rubbing a tiny bit of dirt off the bright white toes of his kicks. "I know I wasn't so nice yesterday about the Shine-A-Thon Showcase, Karma. But . . . I'm really happy you're our director. I know you're gonna make it awesome."

Oh, right. I'd been so busy worrying about Crash's song, I'd forgotten for a second that I was our director. And right now, I didn't feel so awesome about that. "I don't know," I said to Crash. "Switch said being a director's all about making decisions. And so far, I haven't made any." I looked down at my own sneakers. "There's just so much pressure, and I'm worried that I might make the wrong choice." I sighed, remembering all my friends waiting for me to make up my mind. "And I think that makes me the worst director ever."

Suddenly, Crash's head snapped up. "What? No way." He shook his head. "You came up with the idea for this whole show. And you organized a bunch of kids to work together to pull it off. I mean, usually we can't even decide what game to play at recess." We both laughed at that.

"But why did everyone listen to me?" I asked. "Why did we think we could put on a huge concert in two days?"

It was quiet for a minute while Crash thought. Then, he said, "'Cause everyone downstairs believes in you. They know that when you work hard, you get things done." I smiled as Crash continued, "I know that there's pressure. You got this."

It felt like Opposite Day. Was this Crash, the kid who always got on my nerves, suddenly being nice and making me feel better? I guess maybe I didn't know Crash as well as I thought I did. But talking to him now made me realize that I was ready to make my very first decision as director.

"Crash, I want you to sing your song at the beginning of our concert," I said. "The big open, for the whole show!" Crash's face went from smiles back to fear.

"What? My song? Sorry, no way. Nope. No can do. Nuh uh." Crash shook his head, grabbing his backpack and heading toward the stairs.

"Wait, why not?" It was such a good song, and everyone was going to love it at the Shine-A-Thon Showcase!

"I told you, it's not ready," Crash said. "I've never sung my original songs for anyone. What if no one likes it? What if they laugh at me? What if I'm the worst songwriter ever?"

Crash was breathing fast. He was starting to

sweat. He looked like I did when I ran up here to write in my journal. "Crash, your song is great. It's better than great—it's awesome!" I kept talking, looking for the right word. "No, better than awesome—wait, what's better than awesome?"

He cracked a smile when I said this. "Maybe . . . magnificent?"

"Magnificent!" I cheered, and we both laughed. "And when you sing it, you're doing what you love and having fun, right?" He nodded. "Well then, that's what makes you shine. That's what the Shine-A-Thon Showcase is supposed to be all about."

Crash didn't seem convinced. He was still too nervous to share his original songs with our neighborhood, and I didn't know how to convince him. But then I remembered something. "Y'know, someone smart told me something recently." Crash perked up when I said this, curious. I grabbed his arm and looked him right in the eyes. "I know that there's pressure. You got this."

He thought about this for a second. Then he grinned. "Waaait a minute. I just said that to you!" Crash smirked that smirk that totally got on my nerves. "Does that mean you think I'm smart?" Of course, Crash couldn't not be annoying for more than a few minutes.

"Just get downstairs so we can rehearse," I said, shooing him toward the steps. We both started walking back down into the chaos, but then Crash stopped and turned back around to look at me.

"Thanks, Karma," he said, meaning it.

"Thanks back," I said, meaning it, too.

CHAPTER 7

But when we walked downstairs, me and Crash saw that in the time since we'd been gone, things had become a total mess! I looked around the Community Center to see chaos in every direction. Over on the stage, Demi Ray and Sam were arguing about dance moves.

"No, we need to do my one-handed cartwheel thingy here!"

_"Nuh uh," Demi Ray snapped back angrily. "We need to do my turny, twisty thing!"

Behind them Winston was still painting the set—but it wasn't going very well. There was more paint dripping everywhere, and for some reason he was painting everything bright orange.

"Uh, Winston?" I heard Chris asking. "What's with all the orange?"

Winston slopped another giant splat of orange paint on the set. "Don't question my process, Chris."

Over by the costumes Carrie and Danny were tugging back and forth on the purple feather jacket. They were arguing.

"No, I wanna wear it!"

"No, me! I wanna wear it! You wear the astronaut helmet!" Carrie said with an angry flip of her ponytail.

Meanwhile, Keys was still frantically looking for his screwdriver, racing through the room looking under, in, and behind every possible thing. "Has anyone seen a screwdriver? It's red, and lucky, and I need it right now!"

In the middle of it all, Switch was looking at her clipboard, her face full of worry. It seemed like everything for the Shine-A-Thon Showcase was falling apart. Then, she looked up and saw my face. She smiled with relief. "Karma!"

I smiled back and stepped up onto the stage. "Everybody! Everybody, listen up!" I shouted.

"We have a show, and it's tomorrow," I said. "And we have a lot to do to pull it off!" My friends started to look around at one another. "We can't fight and argue—we have to work together." I saw Danny and Carrie drop the jacket they'd been fighting over, both realizing how silly it was to be fighting over feathers.

"I know that we might disagree sometimes," I nodded, turning to Demi Ray and Sam. "But we all want the same thing. We want to put on a show for our neighborhood. And we want every single person here to have a chance to shine."

"So it's time to make some decisions," I said. "And I know our first one: Crash wrote a new song, and he's going to sing it at the start of the show!"

Everyone turned to look at Crash, who rubbed his arm awkwardly. "Really? Crash?" Carrie said. "I've never heard one of his songs before."

I even saw Switch and Winston give each other a look. I could see that they didn't feel confident about my choice. But after my talk with Crash, I wasn't worried about making the wrong choice anymore. I knew this was the right one.

"Crash has got this. The song is amazing, and you'll all hear it tomorrow." I smiled at Crash, who smiled right back. "Listen, if we're ever gonna pull this off, we need to trust each other. We need to believe in each other. And . . . I believe in Crash and his song."

As I spoke, I could see Winston and Switch start to nod. Soon, Chris, Demi, and Carrie were clapping. By the time I finished, the room exploded in the sound of cheers. Everyone was clapping for Crash! "Woohoo! Go Crash!"

"See?" I smiled and nudged him with my elbow. "I knew they'd agree with me." Then I added with a grin, "I'm always right." Crash rolled his eyes at me, but he also smiled. I could tell he was proud.

"Now c'mon, everybody!" I yelled. "We have a show tomorrow—we gotta get back to work!"

♪ ♫ ♩

That afternoon, things started to change. With that first big choice behind me, I realized it wasn't so hard to make decisions— it was actually kind of fun! Especially when I remembered why we were doing all this in the first place. If the point was for all of us to shine, in our own way, then we didn't have to choose one dance move or another.

"Demi Ray, you do your turny-twisty—and Sam, you should totally do your one-handed cartwheel thingy!" I told my friends, and they started working together to make each of their moves into one dance routine.

"And Danny, Carrie—what if we make purple feather jackets for both of you?"

Carrie and Danny smiled and nodded. "I love that idea!" Danny said. "But I've got an even better one—let's make matching feather jackets for everybody!" A perfect compromise!

Even Winston was inspired by the purpose behind Shine-A-Thon. "I was thinking orange before," he explained to me. "But instead of one color, we should do every color—to represent all of us!" Winston held up a canvas that was streaked with lots of awesome colors—all the colors of the rainbow.

"Yes, that's amazing, Winnie!" I loved it so much. I gave him a hug, and Switch came into our hug and squeezed us both, too.

"You did it, Karm. This show is gonna be so cool!"

I nodded. "I think it might be." I couldn't wait for Hansberry Heights to see what we were creating—and how bright we were all gonna shine together.

CHAPTER 8

The next morning, I woke up before my alarm. I could barely sleep! I was so excited about our dress rehearsal—our last practice before the show happened tonight. But even though I was up early, Switch was already waiting for me on the stoop as I took the stairs, two at a time. "Good morning, Producer!"

"Good morning, Director!" Switch said, wiggling her clipboard at me. "Dress

rehearsal day," she said. "This is our first time doing the whole show from start to finish!"

"We got this," I said confidently. "We have everything covered—the costumes, the dance moves, even the puppets. We haven't forgotten anything!"

"AHEM! What about me?" Suddenly Keys appeared behind us, still dragging his wagon of pickle chips. And like usual, he was butting his way into our conversation. Before I could ask him why he was following us, he pulled out a really funny looking machine and held it up to my backpack. I know Keys's inventions are all funny looking—but seriously, this was the weirdest one I'd ever seen! It looked sort of like a vacuum, but at the end of it, there was a big nose! The giant mechanical nose sniff sniff sniffed at my backpack.

"Can I help you?" I tugged my bag away from the nose. "What are you doing? And what is that?"

"It's my Screwdriver Sniffer!" Keys explained. He held up the weird machine as it sniff sniff sniffed the air again.

Me and Switch both started giggling uncontrollably. "Screwdriver Sniffer?!"

"It's an invention that'll help me find my lucky screwdriver!" Keys explained. "I'll just let it sniff sniff sniff . . . and pretty soon, it'll sniff it out!" But just then, the machine started to shake and rattle. There was definitely something wrong with that thing.

"But since I don't have my screwdriver—" Before Keys could finish his sentence, the invention fell into pieces! "I . . . can't really keep it together." Keys sighed and shook his head. "I have to find my screwdriver fast, or I'm never going to be able to finish the Pickle Powered Shine Blaster for the show!"

Even though his weird invention had just sniffed me, I felt really bad for Keys. I don't know how I'd feel if something that I loved was missing—especially if it was the thing that helped me do what I love. It'd be like losing my journal! I pulled Keys into a hug.

"We'll help you find it."

Switch agreed. "We'll look for your lucky red screwdriver everywhere."

That made Keys cheer up a little bit. He smiled at us, then munched on another handful of pickle chips. When I rolled my eyes, he shrugged. "I told you, pickle chips are brain food—they'll help me remember where my screwdriver is!"

"Well just so you know, it's not in my backpack,"
I said. "So you don't have to go sniffing around
there anymore."

♪ 𝄞 ♪

When we got to the Community Center,
everything was ready for our dress rehearsal.
There were chairs set out for our audience to sit
in, and the Center was decorated with streamers,
balloons, and twinkly lights.

Just then, Winston walked up to us, splattered
in even more paint than usual. It looked like
he'd been up all night painting! "I'm finished!" he
said, smiling at me and Switch. He pointed and
we turned to see that he was done painting
the set. It looked amazing—like a swirl of
rainbow colors bursting across the stage. It
totally represented all of us.

"Now, I'm gonna go nap for a million years,"
Winston said. And with a yawn he walked over

to Mateo's pile of puppets and curled up next to one, falling right to sleep.

Switch and I both giggled at Winston, but we couldn't focus on his silliness now. We had to start our dress rehearsal! Switch took her walkie-talkie and announced that we were going to start practicing soon. "Alright, places, everybody! Lights, sound—get ready. Dancers, in position. Crash, you're up first with your new song!"

As Switch and I watched from the audience, the lights went down low, and everything went quiet. It was so dark, I couldn't see anything! But then Sabiya flipped a switch and a bright spotlight turned on. It took a second, but eventually Crash walked out onto the stage and into the spotlight. He stepped up to the mic, and cleared his throat.

"Um, hi. This song, uh . . . well, this song is something I wrote." Crash looked really nervous. Like, really, really nervous. He was even sweating again. "It's about, um, what it feels like for me to be up on stage doing something I love."

Switch, now behind her DJ deck, dropped a beat, and waved her hand to signal Tommie to start playing along on his saxophone. Crash looked to either side of the stage, almost like he was planning to run. He was sweating more and more. But then, he opened his mouth and started to sing.

"*Shine, shine, sh— IIIIEEE!*" Crash stopped, halfway through the first line of his song. It was like he let out a squeak, instead of singing the note he was supposed to. He covered his mouth with his hands, embarrassed.

"Uh . . . lemme try that again." Crash gestured to Switch and Tommie and they shrugged, starting the song over again. Crash took a deep breath, and opened his mouth to sing.

But nothing came out. Crash wasn't singing. He was trying, but no matter what he did, the

sound wouldn't come. I felt so bad for him. He wanted to sing, but something wouldn't let him!

"Ummm, let's take a quick break," Switch said nervously, stopping the beat. Sabiya flipped another switch and all the lights in the Community Center came back on. I saw Crash rush off the stage and out the back door of the Center. I nodded to Switch. "I'm gonna go check on him."

Outside, Crash was kicking some pebbles near

the basketball court. He was talking to himself, and I could see he was really upset. "C'mon, Crash!" I heard him say. "You messed up. You did it all wrong!"

"Um, Crash?" I interrupted, and he looked up at me.

"I know I messed up, Karma, okay? I get it. I'm gonna ruin the Shine-A-Thon Showcase," Crash said with a sigh. It was like he was expecting me to be angry at him. But I just wanted to know what was wrong.

"I don't care about that," I said, pulling Crash to a bench by the court. "I just wanna make sure you're okay. You could sing yesterday—what changed?"

Crash shook his head. "It was different yesterday. It was just you and me. But up there on that stage, with those lights, and everyone looking at me?" Crash sighed again. "I was so nervous about singing my *own* song for everybody. I've never shared something I wrote with so many people and . . . I just couldn't do it."

I nodded. "That happens to me, too. Stage fright." I knew how Crash felt. It could be really scary to be up on stage, singing something new when you weren't sure if people were gonna like it.

"So, you're probably mad you chose me to start the whole show, huh?" Crash said, his voice growing sad. "I disappointed everybody."

"Nuh uh, Crash. You were a little scared—so what? That doesn't mean your song isn't great."

Crash cracked a smile. "Don't you mean . . . magnificent?"

I rolled my eyes and laughed. "Right. Magnificent." He laughed with me. "I believe in you, and that's not gonna change. We'll all help you with your stage fright. You got this." We high-fived, and Crash seemed a lot happier.

Just then, Switch popped her head out the back door and called my name. "Karma! Chris needs your help deciding which kinda burp to do on the letter G!" Crash and I laughed again, and I got up and left him on the bench.

But as I walked back into the Community Center, I started getting nervous. I know I helped Crash feel better, but the truth was I was still worried about our show. Could Crash's song really be the big open we needed to make the perfect concert? Could we help him get past his stage fright to sing it? Could we really pull this off?

We only had a few hours left to figure it out.

CHAPTER 9

When rehearsal stopped for lunch, me, Winston, and Switch did what we always do—we headed to the Duet Diner for our favorite purple scones. Chef Scott owns the diner, and he's also the one who came up with the super-special, super-secret recipe for purple scones. They're crunchy on the outside, soft on the inside, buttery, blueberry'd, crumbly, salty, sweet, and basically the most delicious thing in the whole world. And after the morning we'd had, all three of us felt like a purple scone might be the only thing that could cheer us up.

While we waited for our scones to come, Switch checked her clipboard. "Well, the good news is that we finally have the dance moves done," she tried, but I shook my head.

"Except Sam wants everyone to do a one-handed cartwheel—and Sam's the only one who can do that!"

"Wellll, the costumes are almost finished," she said, trying again.

"Yeah . . . but who knew that Mateo would be so allergic to feathers?" Winston moaned and put his head down on the diner table.

"Then there's our biggest problem"—Switch looked up at me nervously—"Crash."

Winston moaned again, head still on the table. "I forgot about Crash!"

"Karm, I know you love his song . . . but are

you sure he's up for starting our whole show? He wasn't able to sing it once today."

Switch was right. We had tried and tried to help Crash sing and get over his stage fright—but nothing we did made him feel any better about performing his new song for so many people. We tried blindfolding him, so he couldn't see the audience. Nope! We tried spinning him around and around and around before he started singing, so he was too dizzy to even be nervous. That didn't work either. We tried telling him to picture everyone wearing a unicorn costume. That just made him burst out laughing!

Switch tapped her pencil on the clipboard. "Do you think . . . maybe . . ." She locked eyes with Winston before they both finally blurted out:

"We should cut Crash from the show?"

I couldn't believe it. My besties wanted to take Crash out of the show? The show that we'd all been working so hard on? Crash would be heartbroken. There's no way I could ever, ever do that to him. But before I could tell them that I'd never cut Crash, Chef Scott swung through with a giant pile of purple scones.

"Eyy, my favorite customers!" He cheered, placing the plate on the middle of our table. "Purple scones—and these are on the house!"

We all grabbed scones and took big, crumbly bites. They were delicious! We all talked with our mouths full. "Ooh! Thanks, Chef Scott!"

"Of course! It's the least I can do. You three are putting on the biggest show ever for our neighborhood tonight!" Chef pulled two tickets from his apron. "Who needs MC Grillz? We got Karma, Winston, and Switch!" That was nice of Chef to say, but it also made me feel nervous.

"Wow . . . I didn't know you were coming!" I said with a nervous laugh.

Switch gulped and leaned over to tell me,

"Sabiya and Megan said we're sold out on the website—it sounds like the whole neighborhood's coming!" I guess I'd forgotten just how many people that meant would be there for our show.

"Uhhh . . . thanks, Chef! But y'know, it's just a little show," I said.

"Ho ho, that's not what I heard!" Chef Scott laughed as he walked back to the counter. "Chris was in here earlier, talkin' 'bout puppets, and costumes, and some sorta fire-breathing robot dragon?" When he said that, I could hear squeals of excitement from around the diner.

Mr. Crawford and Ms. Washington, who were drinking coffee in the corner, said that they were counting down the hours 'til the show. "I'm comin', Karma—and I'm gonna bring my dancin' shoes!" Ms. Washington shouted to me, shimmying her shoulders.

"I can't wait, either!" our teacher, Mr. Singal, said. "I was so sad when MC

Grillz canceled on us—but this is gonna be even better!"

All around the diner, me, Switch, and Winston saw other folks nodding and agreeing. Time froze as I looked at all of their faces, and I started to hear my heartbeat in my ears again.

"See, Karma?" Switch whispered as the crowd continued to chatter around us. "Everyone's coming tonight. And they're expecting something better than MC Grillz!"

"We have to give it to them," Winston agreed.

"And that might mean . . . not having Crash in the show."

This decision was so big, and I had no clue what choice to make. I wanted to have the very best show possible—especially if all of Hansberry Heights was gonna be there! But could I really do that to Crash?

"Um, I gotta go," I said to Switch and Winston, scooting out of our booth and leaving my half-finished scone on the table. I had too much on my mind, and I didn't know what to do. I had to go home and work it out in my journal.

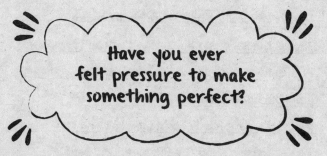

Have you ever felt pressure to make something perfect?

'Cause that's how I feel right now. The Shine-A-Thon Showcase is tonight and I really want it to be great for our neighborhood. If we can't have MC Grillz, I want us to have a night that's just as special!

But I didn't realize people were expecting so much from us! They want music, and dancing, and puppets, and dragons—and they want it to all be perfect! But everything's going wrong—especially Crash's new song. Switch and Winston think if we let him try to sing it, his stage fright might ruin the whole show . . . but is it really the right choice to tell him he can't perform with us?

♫ I don't know what to do, I'm really upset

This is the hardest choice that I've had to make yet

How can we ever live up to what the neighborhood expects?

We gotta make hard choices if we wanna be perfect

I love Crash's song, I believe he can do it

But the fact is, he hasn't really proved it

I know Shine-A-Thon is on the line

But wasn't the point for ALL of us to shine?

My friends think Crash's fears might ruin the show

They're probably right, but I don't know

This has gotta be perfect! We all gotta shine, but . . .

I think maybe Crash won't make the cut. ♪ ♫

Back in my room, I sighed and closed my journal. I had to cut Crash's song . . . even though I didn't want to. It was the only way to put on the perfect show that our neighborhood was expecting.

I got out my tablet and typed a message to Switch. *Okay, you're right. Let's cut Crash's song from the show.*

CHAPTER 10

As we walked back to the Community Center that afternoon, Switch nodded when she crossed off Crash's name. "I know it was a hard decision, Karma," she said sadly. "But I think you made the right choice. We want this show to be perfect, right?"

I nodded. But I didn't really feel like I'd made the right choice. I didn't feel good at all. And I felt even worse when we opened the doors of the Community Center.

The first thing I saw was a pile of purple feathers. Like, a gigantic pile of purple feathers. Switch and I looked at each other, confused.

"Uhh... what's going on?" I asked the feathers. I don't know why I expected a response... but then one came.

"We might've used the wrong glue on the jackets," said a muffled voice from inside the purple pile. Then, Danny's head suddenly poked out of the feathers. "So now all our feather jackets... are regular jackets." Carrie popped her head out of the feather pile, too, and shrugged, holding up our now very boring-looking regular jackets. I sighed—that was bad, but it wasn't even close to the worst news I was gonna get.

Just then, Chris walked by, guzzling a giant bottle of soda. "Uhh... Chris? You okay?"

He didn't look at me—he just kept chugging his soda 'til it was all gone. Then, he turned to me, panic on his face. "I can't burp! I can always burp—but today, it's like nothing will come out!" He opened his mouth to try and burp the ABCs, but he was right. No burps at all!

I covered my eyes with my hands. "Oh no," I groaned. "This can't get any worse."

"Yes it can!" Suddenly Keys was up in my grill again. "My screwdriver's still missing! And you promised you'd help me find it!" He looked worried. "Without it, I'm never going to have my Pickle Powered Shine Blaster ready. We won't be able to blast any lights, or sounds, or cool smoke effects!" Keys nervously shoved more pickle chips in his mouth. I looked down at his wagon—it was almost empty! He'd probably eaten a thousand pickle chips in the past few days.

"I'm sorry, Keys." He was right, I had told him I'd help—but with everything else going on, I'd totally forgotten. "I'll come with you right now and we can look for—"

"Karma?"

Just then, through all the chaos, I heard Crash's voice. It sounded hurt. Really hurt. I turned around to see that Crash was looking down at Switch's clipboard. The same clipboard that had his name crossed off, right at the top.

"What . . . what does this mean?" He turned the clipboard around and pointed to the scratch through his name.

"I . . . I wanted to tell you," I started. But I could see that Crash already knew what I was about to say. And his eyes were starting to fill with tears. "I'm sorry, Crash, but—"

"I'm cut. Yeah, I get it, Karma." Crash put the clipboard back down, and picked up his backpack. "Even if I could sing my song, everyone would probably think it's terrible."

I tried to stop him. "No, wait! Stop, Crash! That's not it!"

But he was already pushing open the doors of the Center. He turned back to me and I could see just how betrayed he felt. "You said you believed in me before. But I guess you were right not to. I'm not magnificent. I'm the worst."

He left. In the silence that came after, I sat down in a chair. I basically felt like the most awful person in the world. Switch came up and squeezed my shoulder. "You okay, Karm?" I wasn't. Honestly, I felt like crying, just like Crash. What made me think we could do this? Put on a show as good as MC Grillz's in just two days? I had promised so much, and now I was totally disappointing everyone. My friends, my family, my neighbors. This show was gonna be a disaster.

I was thinking all this when suddenly I heard a super loud CRASH! And then I heard an even louder SPLASH! "Uhh . . . Karma?"

We all turned around to see that a pipe near the ceiling of the Community Center had just broken open. And now water was gushing from it down onto our stage. Our beautiful rainbow set was dripping with water. So were the puppets, the costumes, the lights, everything. Winston was standing in the middle of it, paintbrush in hand. "I think we might have a little problem."

CHAPTER 11

Pretty soon Mr. Crawford arrived with some mops, grumpily mumbling about the mess. He called over Chris and Carrie to help him clean it up, to which Carrie responded, "Ewwww! I would never!" Mr. Crawford handed her a mop anyway.

Meanwhile, me and Switch looked at all the damage. The stage was ruined, and so were the costumes. Winston's beautiful set had gone from rainbow to rained out, a muddy brown mess of colors. Mateo was trying to delicately dry his poor puppets with his tee shirt. Every single thing we'd planned for the show was now covered in water.

Switch tapped her clipboard nervously, trying to think of solutions. "Um . . . maybe we could fix this with a couple rolls of paper towels?"

I sighed. "More like a couple hundred."

She tried again. "We could make it an underwater-themed show? Then it would make sense for everything to be wet!"

But I just shook my head. "This is all my fault, Switch. Why did I think we could ever pull this off?"

Switch tried to cheer me up, "It's okay, Karma," she said. "We'll think of something!" But it was no use. Nothing was gonna make me feel better.

"I'm gonna go," I said, picking up my backpack and walking out of the Center. I had to get out what I was feeling on the page. I needed to write it down in my journal.

I walked to the park, to a grassy spot under a tree near the chess tables. This was my favorite place—it was quiet, and peaceful, and I could think. Best of all, from here I could see my whole neighborhood block. It was lit up, sunlight bouncing off the rooftops. I took out my pen and my journal and started to write.

Have you ever felt like you disappointed someone?

Well, I feel like I disappointed everyone. All my friends

believed in me when I told them that we could make the

Shine-A-Thon Showcase the most amazing concert ever.

And they all worked so hard, and used all their talent, to

help me make it happen. But of course, I messed it all up.
I made all the wrong choices. I let everything fall apart,
and I wasn't a good leader. I let everybody down . . .
especially Crash.

All we have now is wet costumes, wet puppets . . .
We don't even have a stage to perform on!
I wanted things to be perfect . . . and now, they're the
opposite of that. I did all this 'cause I wanted my friends
to shine. And now, none of us are going to be able to.

    The Shine-A-Thon Showcase, I thought we had it
    handled
    Didn't ever think we'd go from shinin' to canceled
    When we started, I just wanted to show all of our
    talents
    And I knew that together, we were up to the
    challenge

    The whole point of the Shine-A-Thon is shinin'
    Every kid shines brighter when together we're

grindin'

Now everything's ruined, it was gone in a splash

But what's really messed up is what I did to Crash

I felt the pressure to be perfect, from the start
to the end

But I don't care about perfect, I care about my
friends

I gotta make things right, I gotta right this wrong

There's gotta be a way for the show to go on!

I stopped writing my rhymes. But not because the song was finished... Because a new melody started running through my head.

"Shine, shine, shine! Shine brighter than the sun! / Together, we're better, all of us over one! / We are starlight, we shine so bright, each of us have our place! / But when we come together you can see us shine from space!"

Crash's song was so catchy—and so good! But I'd never really thought a lot about the words 'til right now. Crash wrote it about that feeling when you're up on stage, doing something you love. But I realized that that's not all the song was saying. I think it also meant that it's okay to shine on your own. But if you really wanna shine your brightest, you need to do it with your friends. They can be there to help you . . . and you can be there to help them. That's the way to shine as bright as a star.

I had promised to believe in Crash, and then I didn't. I was more worried about everything being perfect than being there for my friend.

I shook my head. Who cared if the Shine-A-Thon was perfect? It felt like there was a lot of pressure on us—but really, the whole point of this was to do what we loved, and have fun doing it. That's what shining was all about!

And that's when it hit me. This whole time, I hadn't really been having fun. I'd been stressed, and worried, and thinking about all the different ways I could mess up. And now, I just wanted to have fun with my friends.

I closed my journal and looked back at my neighborhood. The sun was just about to set, and the buildings were starting to glow. My eyes bounced from rooftop to rooftop, watching them glitter. They finally landed on the Center's roof, where Crash and I had stood just yesterday. It glowed brightest of all.

And that's when I had a great idea. No—not a great idea, a *magnificent* idea! "I know what to do!" I cheered as I got up. And then I started running back toward the Community Center. "I know what *we* have to do!"

♪ ♫ ♪

When I pushed through the doors of the Center, I saw that all my friends were still mopping. I ran to the center of the room, breathing fast. "Everybody! I have an idea!"

⭐ ||| ⭐

Winston held up his stinky-looking mop and sniffed it. "Get new mops?" he asked.

I giggled at him. "No, Winnie. I have an idea for how to save the Shine-A-Thon Showcase!" All my friends' faces lit up. I could tell they were just as excited as I was. "But we have to work fast—the show's only an hour away!"

And just like that, I started making choices like a director—but this time, I was having fun. "Winston, get your paint—every color! And Carrie, Danny—I know our feather jackets are wet . . . but I think I may have a cool idea for how to make those astronaut costumes work!" I started giving everyone a job, and they hurried off to get to work.

Then I saw Keys, wheeling his wagon of pickle chips toward the door. "Keys, where are you going? We only have an hour 'til the concert!"

But he just looked up sadly and shook his head. "I can't find my lucky screwdriver. I'm sorry, Karma, but I'm not gonna be able to finish my Pickle Powered Shine Blaster in time."

I looked at Keys and his wagon for a second. I just didn't understand it—he took that screwdriver everywhere with him. How could he not have found it by now?

"Wait a second!" I walked over to Keys's wagon of chips and stuck my hand in, feeling around.

"Hey, hey! Watch it! You're smushin' all my chips!" Keys exclaimed, trying to stop me. But then, I pulled something out of the pile of chips . . . his lucky screwdriver!

Keys gasped, his eyes lighting up. "You found it! You found it!" He looked down at his wagon. "It was in there, the whole time?"

I giggled and handed the screwdriver over. "I should have known it was right under your nose. But for the record," I said, giving Keys a hug, "you don't need a screwdriver to invent. You shine bright, all by yourself." Keys smiled and squeezed me back.

Then, he broke our hug and started running, pulling his wagon as fast as he could. "Wait, what's happening? Where are you going now?" I asked him.

He didn't stop—just turned back to explain, "I'm going to go make you the most awesome pickle powered invention of all time!" We both laughed as he rushed away.

With everyone else gone, I finally turned to Switch. "And I need you to do the hardest thing of all." Switch twisted her face in confusion. "Pull off a concert . . . on the roof."

"Um, the roof?" Switch pointed up at the ceiling. "Like . . . this roof?"

"Yep!" I replied. "'Cause we're not just doing a concert anymore . . . we're doing the Shine-A-Thon Showcase Rooftop Extravaganza!"

"You got it, Karma." Switch grinned. "I knew you'd know just what to do."

But that reminded me that we weren't done handing out jobs. There was something that only I could do to fix the Shine-A-Thon Showcase in time. "Switch, you get everyone ready—there's one last thing I gotta do."

CHAPTER 12

I found Crash sitting on a stoop on my block. He was scrolling on his phone. He didn't look any happier than when he'd left us all at the Center a few hours before. And when he saw me, he looked the unhappiest I'd seen him. Like, ever.

"Go away, Karma," he said, turning on the step to face away from me. "Don't you have a show to be in? . . . A show without me?" Even though I couldn't see his face anymore, I heard Crash's voice crack a little bit when he said that. And it felt awful to see how much I had hurt him.

"There's no show without you." I walked up the steps and sat next to him. "I was wrong, Crash. And I'm so sorry." He didn't move, or turn to face me. I was still talking to his back. But it didn't matter—I just kept going.

"At some point these past few days, I forgot why we decided to do the Shine-A-Thon Showcase in the first place," I explained. "I got so worried about being perfect that I didn't remember that the whole point was to show all of Hansberry Heights the things we love doing, and how much fun we have doing them. It doesn't matter what costumes we're wearing, or what stage we're on . . ." I paused, then added, "It doesn't even matter if we get a little stage fright."

Crash finally turned around. But he still didn't look like he was forgiving me. "I forgot that the Shine-A-Thon was supposed to be about having fun, and shining together. But your song reminded me." Now, Crash cracked a little smile.

"Really?"

"It's a great song, Crash." I smiled back. Then I corrected myself before he could. "I mean, it's *magnificent*." I squeezed his arm. "And I want you to sing it to open our show."

Crash just shook his head. "It's fine, Karma. I forgive you. But that doesn't change that I'm still gonna get stage fright when I go up there and try to sing." Crash looked out at the passing cars as the sunlight started to fade and afternoon turned into night. "What if, as soon as I get up on stage and start singing my new song, everyone thinks it's terrible? Thinks *I'm* terrible?" He sighed. "I just feel so much pressure. Like I'm all alone."

"Well . . . what if you weren't all alone?" I grinned, nudging him. "What if we all sang with you, and helped you shine?"

"Really, you'd do that? That would be amazing!" Crash's face lit up when I told him my idea.

"Of course. You're our friend." I high-fived him. "You're *my* friend."

But we didn't have time for any more talking. Judging by the sun, the Shine-A-Thon was gonna start any second! "Now c'mon—enough mushy stuff. We gotta get to the roof!" I tugged on Crash's arm as I rushed down the steps.

"Um, excuse me?" Crash yelled as I raced ahead of him down the block. "Did you just say the roof?!"

CHAPTER 13

Crash and I ran all the way back to the Center and took the stairs two at a time to get up to the roof. And when we opened the door . . .

"I can't believe it," I said. I was seriously shocked.

"Whoaaaaaaa," was all Crash could say, his eyes wide.

Up on the roof, all our friends had pulled off the

most amazing transformation ever. Carrie and Danny were handing out astronaut helmets to all our friends. Sam and Demi Ray were getting the stage ready for their fire dance moves. Sabiya, Megan, and Tommie were carrying all the instruments, mics, and speakers into place. Mateo had cleaned off all his puppets, and even Chris was burping again! What used to be an old, boring concrete roof now had chairs, and lights, and decorations—it was a whole outdoor concert arena!

I turned to see that Winston had even painted the wall behind our stage, creating a brand-new set. This time, he'd painted it to look like a rainbow galaxy. It looked like the most beautiful painting of the sky, and it had a colorful starburst exploding from the center. I was so happy, I thought I might cry.

And just when I thought it couldn't get any more amazing, the growing darkness on the roof was suddenly lit up by an

incredible spray of rainbow laser lights. They spread across the entire block! They looked like twinkling stars. Where was that light coming from?

"Ahem." I turned around to see Keys, proudly holding up his Pickle Powered Shine Blaster in one hand and twirling his lucky screwdriver in the other. "You like it?"

"I love it." I gave Keys the biggest hug. "It might just be your best invention ever."

"See?" Keys said with a laugh. "I toldya pickle chips are brain food."

Just then Winston and Switch came up to me. "So, Karm? What do you think?" I couldn't even talk—I just pulled them both in for the biggest group hug ever.

"It's shinin'—just like us."

We all cheered—the Shine-A-Thon Showcase was officially back on! And we were just in time—'cause right then, people started coming up the stairs and walking out onto the roof. Mr. Crawford and Ms. Washington came first, followed by Mr. Singal and Chef Scott. I saw Winston's mom and his abuelita, Switch's dad, and Sabiya's sister!

Then I saw my parents come through the door. They were already cheering, and they were even wearing matching shirts with my face on them. I didn't know it was possible to feel as cool as MC Grillz—with my own tee shirt!—and so embarrassed of my parents at the same time.

Seeing the audience take their seats, Switch got all of us to our places to start the show. And that's when I noticed Crash—looking more nervous than ever.

"Karma, I don't think I can do this. You know,

★ 124 ★

actually, I *know* I can't do this." He was talking super-fast and sweating again. "You were right, the show shouldn't start with my song. The show shouldn't have my song in it at all. Maybe Chris'll start with burping the ABCs instead?"

But I just shook my head. "No way, Crash. We're singing your song." I looked around at all my friends, and they nodded. "Your song is what the Shine-A-Thon is all about. And it's magnificent."

I put my arm around Crash as I heard the crowd start to clap and cheer for us. "Plus, you're not doing it alone," I smiled and pointed back at all our friends. "We're gonna shine, together."

Crash nodded, worry leaving his face. Switch dropped the beat and Tommie started playing the saxophone as we all walked out onto the stage. As he stepped up to the mic, Crash gulped. I didn't know if his stage fright was gonna stop him from singing again. But then he looked back at me, smiled, and gripped the mic tight.

"*Shine, shine, shine! Shine brighter than the sun! / Together, we're better, all of us over one!*"

Crash was doing it! With us behind him, he didn't feel so alone. He had the support he needed. Joining in, all of us sang with Crash, dancing to Demi Ray and Sam's moves and shimmying in our silly astronaut costumes in front of Winston's space-themed design. "*We are starlight, we shine so bright, each of us have our place! / But when we come together you can see us shine from space!*"

As we kept singing, I looked around in amazement at my friends. We were really doing it! Sure, it wasn't perfect: some of our astronaut costumes were still covered in feathers. Our dance moves were wrong sometimes, and I could hear a flat note or two as we started to sing the chorus. But that didn't matter. What mattered was that we were having so much fun! I looked to Switch, then Winston, and saw that they were having a blast, too. As I looked out at our audience, they cheered and sang along. Behind them, I could see the twinkling neighborhood lights and the rush of cars below. It was beautiful.

But then, I noticed something on the street that wasn't exactly beautiful. Actually, it was sort of confusing. It looked like . . . Was that a giant bus, shaped like a toothbrush? It rolled to a stop right in front of the Community Center, and someone popped out of a door in the roof.

"Hey, y'all havin' a concert? Can I join you?"

If it wasn't happening right that second, I never would have believed it could. MC Grillz was here, in our neighborhood—and he was asking to come up on stage and sing with us!

CHAPTER 14

I was stunned. And when I looked around the rooftop, so was everyone else in Hansberry Heights! MC Grillz had somehow made it to our city—and now he was climbing the last of the stairs up to our rooftop concert!

"Whoa ho, look at this!" he said, impressed. "I heard they were puttin' on a show in Hansberry Heights when mine got canceled—but I didn't know it'd be this cool!"

MC Grillz looked around at all our hard work with amazement on his face. "I love it up here. That painting is fire," he said. Winston looked like he was about to faint. He was so excited!

"And these lights? They're next level!"

Keys patted his Pickle Powered Shine Blaster. "Thanks. Wanna pickle chip?"

"Ooh!" MC Grillz nodded and grabbed some chips from Keys, crunching down on their favorite snack.

"And check out these costumes, and puppets. I love it!" MC Grillz continued through a mouthful of chips. "Whoever organized all this is a real producer." Switch blushed and smiled, totally blown away.

"That's Switch Stein." I pointed to my bestie, hyping her up. "She's the best producer ever—and this isn't the last amazing show she's gonna organize up here on the roof!"

Switch turned to me, eyes wide. "Um, it's not?" I smiled back, encouraging her. Then, she laughed and turned to MC Grillz. "She's right—it's not! We're gonna have all sorts of cool shows up here!"

"Well, y'all are seriously talented!" All my friends were so happy—we were getting compliments from MC Grillz himself!

"Also, that song was dope!" MC Grillz bounced his head to the beat that was still playing. "Who wrote this track?"

Thinking quick, Switch shoved Crash right up to MC Grillz. "He did! His name's Crash Watkins."

"Uh, hi." Crash was completely stunned. He could barely speak. "I— I— I'm your biggest fan!"

"Oh yeah? Well, Imma fan of you." MC Grillz gave him a high five.

"I'm sure glad we finally got my Brush Bus up and runnin'—I would've hated to miss this." He looked around with curiosity. "So who put this whole thing together? It must've been a lot of hard work!"

And right then, it was like time froze. Even though it was happening right in front of me, I still couldn't believe it. MC Grillz, *the* MC Grillz, was here—and he loved the Shine-A-Thon Showcase. Me and my friends had worked so hard, and been through so much to get here. But now even MC Grillz could see us shine.

Before I could even think to speak up and say something to him, I heard the rumble of a growing cheer. All my friends had started chanting my name! "Karma! Karma! Karma!" Winston, Switch, and Crash cleared the way so I could be face to face with my hip hop hero.

"That's me," I smiled, putting out my hand. "I'm Karma Grant."

"Well, *I'm* impressed." MC Grillz shook it. "You really know how to put on a concert," he said with a nod, taking another look around.

"But I didn't do it alone," I said, shaking my

head. "We all did it together." I pulled Switch and Winston into hugs around me. "When we do it together, we all shine."

MC Grillz clapped his hands. "I love that! It's next level!" He called over to Switch. "Yo, can you drop that beat again?"

Switch nodded, thrilled, and dropped the beat on her turntable. As Crash's song began to play again, MC Grillz stepped up onto the stage and waved for all of us to come, too. "Alright now, y'all, start singing!" We all started singing Crash's song again—and MC Grillz started freestyle rapping a brand-new verse.

"When we do it together we all shine, we all rise / Shine so bright in the starry night sky / We're stronger together, we shine brighter as one / Oh, and always take care of your teeth and your gums!"

I giggled at MC Grillz's classic dentist rhymes.

Then, outta nowhere he did the most amazing thing. He tossed *me* the mic! "Take it away, Karma Grant!"

It felt like time froze again as I looked at the mic in my hand, then out at the dancing, cheering audience. Then, I turned and looked back at my crew. Switch and Winston, my besties forever. Keys, my sometimes-annoying little brother who I also happened to love more than anyone. Crash, a frustrating classmate who'd turned into a new friend. I was so proud of us. We had made our dream come true—we were singing, up on stage, with MC Grillz! It wasn't how any of us could've ever imagined . . . but it was the most fun I'd ever had.

I twirled around and pumped the mic up to the sky so the whole city could hear all our voices. We sang together, as loud as we possibly could.

"Shine, shine, shine! Shine brighter than the

sun! / Together, we're better, all of us over one! / We are starlight, we shine so bright, each of us have our place / But when we come together you can see us shine from space!"

FROM CREATOR CHRIS "LUDACRIS" BRIDGES:

"I'VE HAD A LOT OF ACCOMPLISHMENTS IN MY LIFE, ALL OF WHICH HAVE ALLOWED ME TO LEAVE A LEGACY FOR MY DAUGHTERS. THEY HAVE TAUGHT ME SO MUCH AND CHANGED ME FOR THE BETTER. I'M EXCITED TO SHARE KARMA'S WORLD WITH EVERYONE WHO WANTS TO CREATE POSTITIVE CHANGE."